MILO MANARA Story by SILVERIO PISU

Preface by RENATA PISU

THE APE
Illustrated by Milo Manara
Story by Silverio Pisu

Translation courtesy of "Heavy Metal", New York,
Lettering courtesy of John Workman
reproduced with permission.

Preface by Renata Pisu
Translated from the Italian by Jeff Lisle
Edited by Bernd Metz

Published by Catalan Communications
43 East 19th Street
New York, NY 10003

ISBN 0-87416-019-7
Dep. L.B. 26323-1985
First Printing January 1986
Printed in Catalonia (Spain)

PREFACE

That nude woman on the last page of this book is Chiang Ching (appropriately under the inscription «shitty intellectuals»). I am the sister of Silverio Pisu, but I am not responsible for this «Ape» of his. Not in the sense that someone could say: «The sister is interested in China, and the brother... well, you know how he is». As children, possibly. Not now. He read «The Ape» and, right away, he wrote a scenario, and then with the help of Milo Manara, he made it into a comic strip. Therefore, I had nothing to do with it. To make «The Ape» into a comic strip isn't at all a sacriledge then. In China, the Chinese also made it into a comic strip, except that instead of calling him «Ape» they called him Sun Wu-K'ung. And the famous novel that has this monkey as the hero isn't called «The Ape» but «Memories of a Voyage to the West». Arthur Waley, who translated the Chinese work into English, has called it «The Monkey» and before that Einaudi and then Adelphi, who published it in Italy, called it «The Ape» («Lo Scimmiotto»).

All of this foreword is not so as to be intellectual (which Milo says is...) but because I began to have doubts when I re-read the story by Pisu and Manara when it was published as «Alter», and I thought that people might possibly think that it is a fantasy. It's a true story... True in the sense that it is a fantasy —but a real Chinese fantasy. It is not a story that two guys in Milan just dreamed up: a magic ape who can do all kinds of things. People would call them crazy, or at least fanciful, very fanciful. No, it was the Chinese scholar Wu Ch'eng-en (who lived... well, 1506 (?) to 1582 (?)... The dates are approximate because there's some scholar who disputes the authorship of this book, saying that Mr. Wu absolutely never existed) who invented the story when he went to Huai-an in north Kiangsu. (Are you following my thought?) But this also is not true —actually it's quite false— but more probable.

In reality, these are the facts: Wu Ch'eng-en, if he ever existed, inspired legends which have accumulated for centuries around a real episode —the voyage to the West (from China to India) made by the monarch Hsuang Tsang in the 7th century to look for the sacred scriptures, which being Indian, were Buddhist. This is all history and well-documented. But let's forget about this story, not so much because Wu Ch'eng doesn't tell about it in his novel as it appears to be —a great comic undertaking such as Don Quixote would make, but simply because Manara and Pisu have made a comic strip out of Arthur Waley's version, in which he, Waley, had translated only thirty of the at least one hundred chapters in the original by Wu Ch'eng-en. Manara and Pisu stopped at the point where the Ape dies and where he's buried deep inside a mountain. It's like saying: «Mao is dead». But «...and if you want to know how long and in what year and what month he died, you should listen to how it's related in the next chapter». We are hopeful. But here there isn't a next chapter, nothing more of what's to come, no future. In the novel, yes, it goes on.

This is why I said that this nude woman on the tomb/mound/mountain is Ching. You could say that in that place, Manara and Pisu are naming characters, but let me explain. Let's go back to 1961 —a big step forward, considering that the book was written 400 years ago, inspired by stories about an event that happened 1300 years ago. But it is a step back with respect to September and October of 1976 when Mao died, his wife Chiang Ching was arrested and ended up (symbolically?) being sacrificed on the pyre of her mate in the Indian manner. And in China in 1961, the movie theaters were showing a film titled «Sun Wu-k-ung (that is, «The Ape») Drives the Phantom of the Skeleton Away Three Times», and this film is about an episode that is not in the Manara and Pisu adaptation nor is it in the Arthur Waley story... but it is very popular in China. Let me tell you that story: Hsuan Tsang, the Monk who has gone looking for the sacred Buddhist scriptures, is accompanied by the Ape who was released after 500 years to be his companion. In the street they come across the Phantom of the Skeleton who is convinced that he can attain immortality by eating the flesh of Hsuan Tsang. To deceive him, the Phantom tranforms himself into a beautiful woman and accompanies the pilgrims. But the Ape is not fooled and hits him and knocks him out. But the Phantom doesn't give up and now disguises himself as a poor old woman. Again the sly Ape recognizes him and knocks him out again. The next disguise is that of a venerated old man, and the Ape, this time with the help of the gods of the mountain, unmasks the Phantom and throws him out once and for all. Instead of being grateful, Hsuan Tsang accuses the Ape of having senselessly killed two women and a helpless old man and he punishes him. At the end, however, he believes him and pardons him.

Mao went to the movies, perhaps with his wife, and certainly with the great poet,

dramatist, archeologist, etc., Kuo Mo-jo, who, taking his cue from the film spectacle, wrote poetry to Mao. Mao wrote back with another poem, always on the same theme, that is, the Ape theme. Here are Mao's verses:

From the time wind and thunder swept across the earth
a Phantom came out of a heap of white bones.
The monk is a simple spirit, whom one could educate
but the wicked phantom is the source of calamity.
Resolved, the ape raises the heavy mace
and scatters the black powder that thickens over the entire world.
Today we salute with joy, Sun the Ape
because the poisonous fog came back again, even thicker.

Well, who are these characters in the verse? according to Stuart R. Schram, the most authoritative Western expert on Mao, the poetry is interpreted like this (and remember, this is in 1961 when the Soviet-Chinese dispute had just begun): the Monk (Hsuan Tsang) would be Khrushchev, a simple soul, but with re-education, redeemable (at least that's what the Chinese thought in 1961). The Phantom of the Skeleton would be imperialism (or revisionism according to some other commentators). And the ape? The Ape is Marxism-Leninism —the Ape is Mao. I didn't make this up, nor did my brother, not even Milo Manara. This is the interpretation of people who are a lot more serious than we are. For me, however, that nude woman on the last page is Chiang Ching.

Well, I guess no one can say that I haven't given some key to reading this book. I can't read anything without some kind of introduction. To avoid talking about comics, I wish we had here something more straightforward: first one figure speaks, then another —and not all this stuff of factions, worldviews, negotiations, etc. If I read, I read and if I look, I look. But in China, they say reading and writing in the same way: K'an. For them it's never understood if one looks at a book or if one reads it. For me there is a difference. There are books that I look at and books that I read. But the Chinese, writing is making a design and , therefore, looking is «reading looking» or «looking reading». And, one could say (they would say) these picture words are comics— another invention of theirs, as usual.

RENATA PISU.

THE APE
BY PISU AND MANARA
PISU
ONE DAY A BOULDER, SATURATED WITH THE PURE ESSENCE OF EARTH, THE ENERGY OF LIGHT, AND THE EXQUISITE AROMA OF DEWY GRASS WAS FOUND IMPREGNATED, AS IF BY MAGIC. IT HAS BEEN SAID THAT THE EGG IT HARBORED WAS FERTILIZED BY THE WIND.
AND FROM THE EGG, A YOUNG APE OF STONE WAS BORN, PERFECT IN BODY.
HE BOWED DOWN TO THE FOUR CARDINAL POINTS, AND A FAINT GLIMMER EMANATED FROM HIS GESTURE.

THE SPARKLING LIGHT SHONE THROUGH THE FOG, TOUCHED THE SKY, AND OPENED THE GOLDEN DOORS OF THE EMPEROR OF JADE'S CHÂTEAU...

IT GLITTERED FOR A MOMENT...

...AND THEN STOPPED.

GUARDS! CELESTIAL MINISTERS! OPEN THE DOORS OF THE MERIDIONAL SKY AND FIND OUT WHO DARES TO SCRUTINIZE MY INTIMACY!

THE IMPUDENT SLOB... HE SHOULD KNOW TO HAVE RESPECT FOR THE EMPEROR OF JADE.

IT'S BEEN YEARS SINCE THIS GATE HAS BEEN OPENED.
PUSH HARDER! SOON IT WILL BE DAWN AND WE WILL NO LONGER BE ABLE TO FIND HIM IN THE HAZE!

EYE OF 1000 UNIONS ...WHAT DO YOU SEE?
IT'S A YOUNG APE!... HE SEEMS TO BE MISTREATING SOME SORT OF TIGER!

WHO IS THAT SPLENDID YOUNG APE THAT RIDICULES BOTH HEAVEN AND EARTH?
GOOD MORNING, EVERYONE! ISN'T LIFE HERE WONDERFUL? WE HAVE GREENERY AND THE PUREST WATER ANYONE COULD HOPE FOR!
THIS IS FINE FOR NOW, BUT BEYOND THAT CASCADE A BETTER WORLD IS AWAITING US! THE ONE WHO HAS COURAGE ENOUGH TO DISCOVER WHAT IS BEYOND THAT WATERFALL WILL BE OUR LEADER...OUR KING!
OH, OLD AND WISE ONE...DON'T YOU THINK THIS HAS GONE FAR ENOUGH? WE TRAVEL AND TRAVEL IN HOPES OF FINDING NIRVANA, BUT IT'S HOPELESS. THIS HAS BECOME ONE BIG JOKE.
BUT WE MUST TRY, MY CHILD... WE CAN'T STOP NOW. WE WILL NEVER KNOW WHAT IS BEHIND THE WATERFALL UNTIL WE SEE FOR OURSELVES.
YAAAHHH
WHERE IS THE APE OFF TO? DO YOU THINK HE WILL BE BACK?
I PROMISE YOU... HE WILL BE BACK, AND HE WILL BE KING!

WHAT A BEAUTI-FUL PLACE. WE CAN SETTLE HERE.
THIS WILL BE MY KINGDOM!
COME ON! I HAVE FOUND A BEAUTIFUL, SAFE, AND COMFORTABLE CORNER! IT WILL EASILY ACCOMODATE 10,000 OF US!
BUT WHAT ABOUT THE REST OF OUR PEOPLE? WE CAN'T JUST LEAVE THEM HERE TO DIE!
CAN WE TRUST HIM?
GUIDE ME...
SPLENDID!
I'M AFRAID!
IS THE WATER COLD?

MEANWHILE, BACK AT THE EMPEROR OF JADE'S CHÂTEAU...
LOOK AT THEM! THEY ARE SLEEPING WHILE ON DUTY!
Z
Z
WAKE THEM UP AND CUT OFF THEIR HEADS!
OH, IS IT ALREADY MORNING, MY GRACIOUS MASTER?
ONE HUNDRED YEARS HAVE GONE BY WHILE YOU WERE TAKING YOUR LITTLE CAT NAP.
NOTHING CEASES TO AMAZE ME IN THIS KINGDOM OF MINE!
STZAK!
BUT THE LACK OF EFFICIENCY FRIGHTENS ME NONETHELESS!
STAK!
YOU SHOULD HAVE NO PROBLEM WITH THE YOUNG APE THAT ANNOYED YOU ...WE'VE BEEN FOLLOWING HIM, AND... ARGHHH!
AH, WELL DONE, MY DEARS! AND AS FOR THE APE, LET HIM LIVE ON... AS LONG AS IT IS BEYOND THE CASCADE. HOW DOES THAT SOUND TO YOU, MY FLOWERS?
WHAT HAPPENS OVER THERE DOESN'T MATTER TO US. WE LIVE FOR YOU... OUR LIVES ARE YOURS!

NO MORE FRUIT, PLEASE... I'VE HAD MY FILL.
FOR ME?
YES, A NECKLACE MADE OF MIRTH FOR A HAPPY FUTURE.
WHEN DID WE CROSS THE VEIL OF OPALINE WATERS?... IT MUST HAVE BEEN CLOSE TO A HUNDRED YEARS AGO.
THE WRINKLES ON YOUR FOREHEAD ARE GROWING DEEPER AND DEEPER. WHAT IS TORMENTING YOU, KING APE?
LIFE HERE HAS BEEN BLISSFUL... WE HAVEN'T HAD TO DEAL WITH BEASTS FROM THE OUTSIDE WORLD... WE HAVE ALL THE FOOD AND WATER WE NEED, AND TIME HERE GOES SO MUCH SLOWER THAN ON THE OTHER SIDE OF THE WATERFALL.
I DON'T WANT ANYTHING ELSE.
BUT I AM SURE THAT LIFE MUST BE EVEN BETTER BEYOND THE FRUITED TREES THAT THE CRYSTALLINE STREAMS...
HEAVEN MUST FOLLOW!
I'VE HAD ENOUGH!
ENOUGH OF EVERYTHING!
LET'S THROW A PARTY TONIGHT... MAYBE THAT WILL HELP HIM GET OUT OF HIS MOOD.
WHY IS HE SO UPSET?
LAO-TZE HAS GOT SOME INCREDIBLE GRASS.

NOT ANOTHER PARTY! A DAY DOESN'T GO BY WITHOUT A FESTIVAL IN HONOR OF MY NAME, MY THUMB, MY PUG NOSE. I CAN'T WAIT TO ATTEND THE FESTIV-ITIES WHEN THEY HONOR MY SHAGGY ASS!
KING APE, PLEASE DON'T FEEL THIS WAY! COME WITH ME. WE WILL LAUGH... DANCE... MAKE LOVE. WHAT'S WRONG WITH HONOR-ING YOU, OUR BELOVED KING?
YOUR MAJESTY IS VERY DIFFICULT TO KEEP AMUSED.

I KNOW... BUT I CAN'T LIVE MY NEXT 1000 YEARS LIKE THIS.

WHAT KIND OF APE LIVES A LIFE OF LUXURY SUCH AS THIS?

OLD AGE WILL TACKLE ME SOON, BEFORE MY 1000 YEARS ARE UP!

BUT, MY TREASURE... THAT WILL HAPPEN TO ALL OF US!
AND YAMA, THE KING OF DEATH, IS CALLING ME.

IF THAT IS WHAT IS TROUB-LING YOU, THEN RE-LIGION MUST HAVE GONE FROM YOUR HEART... YOU NO LONGER WANT TO BE LIKE US; YOU WANT TO BE IM-MORTAL.
YES, YOU ARE RIGHT... I DON'T WANT TO DIE. I WANT TO LIVE ON FOREVER.

AMONG ALL CREATURES, THREE KINDS ARE PROTECTED FROM THE DOMINATION OF YAMA: BUDDHAS, IMMORTALS, AND THE WISE ONES. THEY ALONE ARE EXEMPT FROM THE MOVEMENT OF THE WHEEL, FROM THE FINAL STAGES OF LIFE— DEATH.

DO YOU KNOW WHERE I CAN FIND THEM? WHERE I CAN BE TAUGHT ABOUT IMMORTALITY?

YOU CAN FIND THEM IN THE ANCIENT GROTTOS OF THE ENCHANTED MOUNTAINS.

SPLENDID! LISTEN TO ME, EVERYONE. TOMORROW I WILL BE LEAVING YOU, OFF TO WANDER LIKE A CLOUD, IN ORDER TO SEARCH FOR THREE SPECIES— BUT EVEN IF I FIND ONLY ONE, I SHALL BE CONTENT.

TOMORROW WE WILL GIVE A LARGE FAREWELL BANQUET IN HONOR OF OUR KING!

I WILL LEARN HOW TO REMAIN YOUNG FOREVER... I SHALL NEVER TEMPT THE FATES AGAIN WITH MY IMPERFECTIONS.

MAGNIFICENT! BRAVO!

THE FOLLOWING DAY...

WHERE IS THE KING?

HE GOT UP VERY EARLY THIS MORNING. HE CUT WOOD AND VINES AND MADE A RAFT FOR HIMSELF...

NOW HE'S OVER THERE... HE'S GOING DOWN THE FALL, FARTHER AND FARTHER AWAY.

TOO BAD... AND WE PREPARED QUITE A FAREWELL FEAST FOR HIM.

TOO BAD... INDEED... BUT IT SHAN'T GO TO WASTE.

THE YOUNG APE WAS FINALLY HAPPY... FOR HE WENT DOWN THE STILL WATERS TOWARDS THE RAPID SEA. AND HE COULD CONTINUE HIS TRIP UNTIL HE FOUND JUST ONE OF THREE TRUTHS...

THE YOUNG APE OF STONE, WHO WAS BORN FROM A MAGICALLY PREGNANT ROCK, UPSET THE EMPEROR OF JADE IN HIS CHÂTEAU OF CLOUDS. HE IS NOW IN SEARCH OF IMMORTALITY BECAUSE WHO WANTS TO DIE WITH ONLY 1000 YEARS OF LEISURE UNDER HIS BELT?! HE WANTS TO LIVE, AND FOREVER IS JUST THE RIGHT AMOUNT OF TIME TO FIT IT ALL IN!

POLITIC?
SFRUTTAMENT
Coca-Cola
GRAN LUPANARE
SESSO
LOVE
SEX
RESTAURANT
OIL
AH! PEOPLE OF THE BRIDGE! DO YOU KNOW WHERE I CAN FIND A BUDDHA OR AN IMMORTAL? ...EVEN A WISE MAN WOULD DO!

WE ARE BUSY FINDING FAME AND GLAMOUR... TRY THE ANCIENT GROTTOS!

I SEARCHED FOR IMMORTALITY TOO, AND LOOK HOW THEY'VE TREATED ME! GO! LOOK IN THE ENCHANTED MOUNTAINS!

HOW LUCKY FOR ME THAT I AM NOT AFRAID OF TIGERS OR WOLVES OR OTHER BEASTS OF LOST LANDS!
AND SO HE ARRIVED AT THE GRAND PARK OF WOOD LIFE...

I DON'T WEAVE PLOTS, I DON'T CHAIN CHAINS. WHEN LIFE IS SIMPLE, IT IS LONG! ON MY ROAD, IMMORTALS PASS AND COMMENT ON YELLOW WRITINGS!
HERE YOU ARE, AT LAST!
IMMORTAL PRIEST! PLEASE TAKE ME AS YOUR DISCIPLE!
BE ON YOUR WAY, FILTHY BEAST! I AM NOT IMMORTAL AND I HAVE NO DESIRE TO BE IMMORTAL!
ARGHHH...THEN WHY DO YOU SING THAT WAY? HEY, WHAT ARE YOU DOING?
MONDO CANE!
OKAY...OKAY... I'LL...AAH!...TELL YOU! AN IMMORTAL WHO LIVES BY MY CABIN TAUGHT ME THAT VERSE! "SING THIS SONG WHEN YOU HAVE WORRIES," HE TOLD ME. I HAVE PLENTY OF WORRIES, SO I SING IT CONSTANTLY!
IF THE IMMORTAL LIVES NEAR YOU, WHY WON'T YOU TAKE HIM AS YOUR TEACHER? YOU CAN LEARN HOW TO LIVE FOREVER!
I HAVE AN OLD MOTHER... MANY SISTERS... I'M WITHOUT A PENNY... I HAVE NOTHING TO EAT... I CUT WOOD AND SELL IT FOR A HANDFUL OF RICE... I HAVE NO TIME FOR MAGIC!
STRANGE, HE NEVER EVEN THANKED ME!...ME! I RID HIM OF A LIFE WITH LITTLE HONOR AND CERTAINLY NO REWARD!

GROTTO OF THE OBLIQUE MOON, THE SACRED TERRACE, AND THE THREE STARS ON THE MOUNTAIN.
DOCTOR IN
MY GOD! WHAT AN IMPORTANT MOMENT FOR ME... BUT I'M REALLY HUNGRY!
I'LL PUT IMMORTALITY ASIDE FOR A MOMENT!
WHO'S THERE?
DOCTO IN
O, MAGIC CHILD, I'M A STUDENT WHO'S COME TO LEARN ABOUT IMMORTALITY. I DIDN'T REALIZE I WAS MAKING ANY NOISE!
I SEE! GOOD. COME IN! THE OLD MAN ASKED ME TO WATCH FOR YOU!
BUT... HOW DID HE KNOW THAT I WAS COMING? CLAIRVOYANCE?
NO, CLOSED CIRCUIT TV!

MASTER, I PRESENT TO YOU THE HUMBLE RESPECTS OF A STUDENT!
A NAME... GIVE HIM A NAME... YOU'LL INTRODUCE YOURSELF THEN... BUT FIRST, THE NAME... THE NAME!
THEY'VE GOT-TEN RID OF RE-LIGION IN SCHOOLS AND THIS IS THE RE-SULT! ANOTHER YOUNG MYSTIC WHO'S COME TO BOTHER US HERE AT THE CONVENT!
HERE! LEAVE THE MASTER IN PEACE! WE'LL THINK OF A RITUAL NAME FOR THIS BEAST!

THERE ARE TWELVE CLASSES OF DISCIPLES. THEY ARE...
...GREAT, BIG, WISE, SKILLFUL, CONFORMING, OCEAN, LIVING, CONSCIOUS, PERFECT, ENLIGHTENED, SINCERE, AND, UH, ATTRACTIVE! YES, ATTRACTIVE!
SINCE YOU ARE OF THE EIGHTH CLASS, YOU MUST HAVE THE WORD "CONSCIOUS" IN YOUR NAME.
WHAT DO YOU THINK OF CALLING HIM CONSCIOUS OF EMPTINESS?
MAGNIFICENT! FROM THIS MOMENT ON, I SHALL BE CONSCIOUS OF EMPTINESS. AND NOW WHAT MUST I DO?
YES! YES! YES! I WILL DO IT! I WILL DO IT!
CLEAN, DUST, REARRANGE, TALK ONLY WHEN QUESTIONED, AND...
STOP MAKING SO MUCH NOISE!
THREE SUMMERS...
THREE WINTERS...
THREE SPRINGS...
LIFE... IS A GREAT WAY... A RIVER!
OH, MAJESTY ...WHAT BEAUTIFUL WORDS!

SCHALAFF
CON-SCIOUS OF EMPTINESS! HOW DARE YOU DISTURB MY LESSON?
LIFE IS A RIVER... A RIVER IS MADE OF WATER...
I'VE SPILLED THE WATER... THUS, HERE IS LIFE!
FINISHED! FINISHED LIKE LIFE!
WHAT SORT OF WIS-DOM DO YOU HOPE TO LEARN FROM ME, CONSCIOUS OF EMPTINESS?
ANYTHING... TEACH ME WHAT YOU WILL!
WHAT WOULD YOU SAY ABOUT NATURAL PHILOSOPHY? CONFUCIUS, LAO-TZE, DUALISM,.. READ THE WRITINGS, RECITE SOME PRAYERS, AND THEN...
WILL I LIVE FOREVER?

AND AFTER QUIETISM THERE IS: TEMPERATE DIET, INERTIA, MEDITATION, ABSTENTION, PROSTRATE AND STANDING YOGA...
BUT WILL THAT MAKE ME IMMORTAL?
HERE ARE THE EXERCISES: GET YIN AND JOIN IT TO YANG, STRETCH THE BOW AND LOAD THE CATAPULT, RUB THE NAVEL, EXHALE...
AND ETERNAL LIFE?
MISERABLE APE! YOU MUST STUDY TO ACHIEVE IMMORTALITY! LIVING IS NOT MADE UP OF BANANAS AND PAPAYAS!!!
VULGAR PRIMATE! THE MASTER IS TERRIBLY UPSET NOW ...WHO KNOWS WHEN HE WILL START TEACHING AGAIN... IT'S YOUR FAULT!... WHAT WISDOM ARE YOU SEARCHING FOR, IF WE MAY ASK?
HAND SIGNALS=SCIENCE OF THE IMMORTALS VERY DIFFICULT TO ASCERTAIN.
THREE FINGERS BEHIND THE BACK...THAT'S CLEAR!
LEAVE THEM TO THEIR HYSTERICS, POOR IDIOTS! I UNDERSTAND THE LANGUAGE OF THE SECRET SIGNS!

THAT NIGHT, THE THIRD EVENING...
PASSING THROUGH THE BACK DOOR...
MASTER... YOU HAVE ORDERED ME BY A SECRET SIGN TO COME TONIGHT...
CONSCIOUS OF EMPTI-NESS?
SO YOU UNDERSTOOD MY MESSAGE, HUH? YOU'RE MORE CLEVER THAN I THOUGHT... WELL, LISTEN...
MIND
SOUL
BREATH
KEEP AND CARE FOR VITAL FORCES.
MAKE PROVISIONS FOR THEM IN YOUR BODY.
I CAN TEACH ONLY THAT.
LOOK AT THE EMBRACE OF THE TORTOISE AND THE SNAKE...
IN THE FLAMES GROWS THE LOTUS OF GOLD...
COMBINE THE FIVE ELEMENTS AND BE WHAT YOU WANT...
BUDDHA OR IMMORTAL.

BY THE WAY, WHAT HAS BECOME OF THE YOUNG APE... THAT AMUSING FELLOW WHO WAS BORN FROM THE EGG OF A STONE?
AMUSING? HE'S REMARKABLE! HE ALREADY KNOWS SEVENTY-TWO TRANSFORMATIONS AND RIDES THE CLOUDS LIKE A REAL COWBOY!
HE WENT TO LEARN ABOUT IMMORTALITY. HE CLAIMS HE NOW KNOWS THE "FORMULA" AND WON'T STOP TALKING ABOUT IT.
AND SIMULTANEOUSLY IN THE GROTTO OF THE OBLIQUE MOON AND THE THREE STARS, ON THE MOUNTAIN OF THE SACRED TERRACE...
YOUNG APE... CONSCIOUS OF EMPTINESS, LET ME SEE A FEW OF THE MAGIC FORMULAS I HAVE TAUGHT YOU!
YES, RIGHT AWAY, MASTER!
ZAP
IS THAT ALL? YOU'LL NEVER BECOME A TRUE AVIATOR OF THE CLOUDS...
...WITH SUCH A SHORT REPERTOIRE!

COME AND LET ME SHARE ANOTHER FORMULA WITH YOU. IT'S CALLED TRAPEZE OF THE CLOUDS, AND IT WILL PERMIT YOU TO FLY ACROSS THE WORLD IN A SINGLE DAY.
FASTER THAN A JET? WONDERFUL!
WHAT DAMNED LUCK THAT MONKEY HAS! IF HE LEARNS TO FLY LOW ENOUGH, HE CAN DISTRIBUTE MESSAGES, LETTERS, AND BROCHURES. WHY, HE'LL BE IN BUSINESS FOR LIFE!
I WANT THE MASTER TO TEACH ME THAT ONE ABOUT TURNING BARK INTO FISH. MAYBE EVENTUALLY, I COULD PUT UP SAIL, GO TO THE RIVIERA, AND OPEN A RESTAURANT.

THANKS AGAIN, DEAR MASTER.
I'LL SCRUTINIZE IT THOROUGHLY.
I WOULDN'T MISS IT!
I'LL TELL HER!
MY PLEASURE. NOW STUDY THAT LAST FORMULA!
I'LL SEE YOU TOMORROW?
MY BEST TO YOUR MOTHER!

IT'S YOUR FAVORITE STUDENT, MASTER! HE'S BEEN SHOWING OFF ALL THE DIFFERENT FORMULAS YOU TAUGHT HIM!

CONSCIOUS OF EMPTINESS! I DIDN'T TEACH YOU THOSE MAGICAL FORMULAS IN ORDER FOR YOU TO OPEN A SIDE SHOW!
BUT, SIN-CERELY, I...

SIGH...YOU HAVE BEEN A STRANGE STUDENT... HERE YOU ARE IM-MORTAL WITH ALL THE TRANSFORMATION SECRETS UNDER YOUR BELT. YOU COULD FLY FARTHER THAN ANY AIR-LINE COMPANY, INCLUD-ING TWA, AND YET YOU STAY HERE AND SHOW OFF TO THESE MORTALS! YOU MUST GO-DON'T FORGET YOU ARE A KING AND YOUR PEOPLE NEED YOU!

YOU MUSTN'T STAY HERE ANY LONGER!
WHERE WILL I GO?

HARK! THE PEOPLE ARE CALLING FOR ME! I MUST GET TO THE GROTTO OF THE HANGING WATER!

GOOD-BYE, O MASTER! GOOD-BYE!

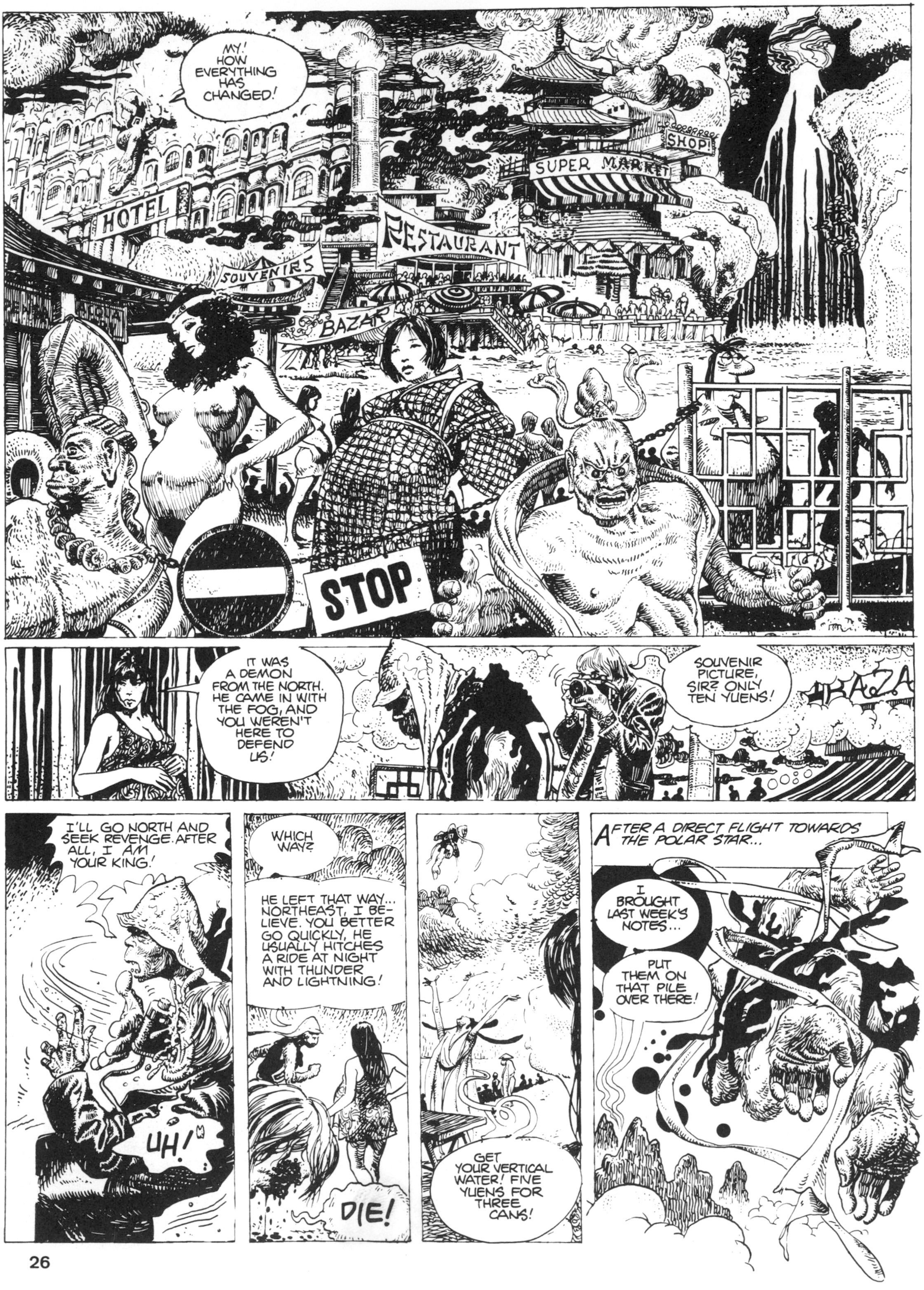

MY! HOW EVERYTHING HAS CHANGED!
HOTEL
RESTAURANT
SUPER MARKET
SHOP!
SOUVENIRS
BAZAR
STOP

FIVE OFFERINGS OF SILVER? THAT'S NOT VERY MUCH!
A HOLOCAUST!... NO...NO...NO!.. I DON'T WANT TO GET INVOLVED!
AND WHAT ABOUT THE HIDING PLACE? WE MUST CLOSE UP THAT DAM SURREPTITIOUSLY!
WE CAN'T IGNORE A MESSAGE LIKE THAT! I'LL TAKE A LOOK! BY THE WAY, DID YOU KNOW THAT THE ROMAN EMPIRE FELL?
MEETING OF THE COUNCIL WILL NOW COME TO ORDER!
THE DOCTOR IS OUT... ERRR... RATHER, IN A MEETING.
GO AND TELL YOUR BOSS THAT A MASTER FROM THE HANGING WATER GROTTO IS HERE. I'VE COME TO SETTLE UP WITH HIM!
GREAT KING... WHAT A TERRIBLE THING!
I'VE HEARD SO MUCH ABOUT THE APES, AND HERE IS THEIR KING. HE DOESN'T SCARE ME. ERRR, IS HE ARMED?
HE'S OVER THERE... UNARMED!
HE DOESN'T HAVE ANY WEAPONS? SO, HE KNOWS MAGIC! QUICK, BRING ME MY EQUIPMENT!

THE YOUNG APE, NOW IMMORTAL, IS ABLE TO TRANSFORM EACH AND EVERY HAIR ON HIS BODY, IF HE IS SO INCLINED. AND SO HE WAS, FOR HE RIPPED OUT A SMALL TUFT OF HAIR... CHEWED IT QUICKLY, AND...

AYYYEEEE HAAA

THE UNITED VILLAGE...

...BUT NOW, MY LITTLE ONES, THE TIME OF BANQUETS AND MARDI GRAS IS OVER. WE MUST LEARN TO DEFEND OURSELVES; NO DOUBT THE REPRISAL WILL BE A MESSY ONE.

IF YOU TEACH US WELL, WE WILL LET YOU IN ON A LITTLE SECRET. THERE IS A CITY 200 MILES FROM HERE...
...THAT HAS CAVERNS FULL OF WEAPONS.

I DON'T NEED TO BUY WEAPONS... I STEAL THEM TELEPATHICALLY.
YES, GOOD KING. BUT IF YOU WANT THEM, WE CAN GET THEM FOR YOU.
AND AT A GOOD PRICE, TOO!

WELL, THEN, GO ON, LITTLE APES. BRING BACK ENOUGH AMMO FOR EVERYONE!

SWEET KING, OUR DELEGATION HAS ARRIVED IN ORDER TO PAY HOMAGE TO YOU, THE GREATEST OF ALL WHO HAVE REIGNED.
YOUR 47,000 WARRIORS ALSO DESERVE A TRIBUTE...
...WHICH WE WILL PAY EVERY SEASON IN EXCHANGE FOR A PROMISE...
...THAT YOUR PEOPLE WILL NEVER ATTACK OUR FAIR VILLAGE.
ATTACK? BUT WE WOULD NEVER ATTACK WITHOUT REASON!
EXCUSE ME, YOUR MAJESTY, BUT WHAT MY FRIEND MEANT WAS THAT YOU SHOULD PROTECT US AGAINST NEIGHBORING BARBARIC TRIBES.
THIS MOUNTAIN OF FLOWERS AND FRUIT IS AS STRONG AS A BRONZE WALL... SO SHALL WE SHAKE ON IT?
YES, YES, WE SHALL PROTECT YOU AS BEST WE CAN. BUT I MUST FIND BETTER WEAPONS. THIS DAGGER IS TOO LIGHT FOR ME!
THAT IS BECAUSE IT IS AN EARTH WEAPON AND YOU ARE NOW IMMORTAL. THE ONLY PLACE YOU WILL EVER FIND A WEAPON WORTHY OF YOU IS AT THE POWERS OF THE SEA.
I'LL GO TO THE PALACE OF THE DRAGON NEAR THE EASTERN SEA. HE'LL KNOW WHERE I CAN OBTAIN A WEAPON WHICH WILL BE ADEQUATE FOR ME.
ANOTHER VOYAGE? THIS APE CAN'T STAY STILL FOR A MINUTE!

AND SO, THE YOUNG APE OF STONE, WHO HAS LEARNED IMMORTALITY, MAGIC, AND RELIGION, IS LEAVING IN ORDER TO FIND A WEAPON WHICH CAN BE ADAPTED TO SUIT HIS MOST SPECIAL POWERS.
OF WHAT RACE ARE YOU BORN TO? AND WHY ARE YOU SWIMMING TO THE PALACE OF THE DRAGON OF THE EASTERN SEA?
I AM THE KING OF THE MOUNTAIN OF FLOWERS AND FRUIT, AND I HAVE COME TO MEET THE DRAGON.
YOU MUST GO! I'M WARNING YOU!
VIOLENCE IS NOT NECESSARY. I IMMEDIATELY RECOGNIZED YOU! YOU ARE THE POWERFUL YOUNG APE, BORN FROM STONE, AM I NOT CORRECT? COME IN! AND GENERAL LOBSTER... CORPORAL CRAB!...
...A LITTLE HONOR AND RESPECT FOR THIS GREAT APE!
IT'S SO NICE TO MEET YOU. A LITTLE KISS!
SCIAF
YOU BRUTE!
CAN I OFFER YOU A CUP OF TEA?

I HAVE BEEN TOLD THAT YOU HAVE A GREAT MANY MAGICAL WEAPONS. I AM SEARCHING FOR ONE THAT WILL SUIT MY NEEDS... ALL OF MY NEEDS.
YES, I DO HAVE A BEAUTIFUL COLLECTION! I KEEP THEM BEHIND A DOOR OF SEMIPRECIOUS SHELLS AND STONES.
WHAT DO YOU THINK ABOUT THIS FORK WITH NINE POINTS?
WELL, IT'S VERY BEAUTIFUL BUT TOO LIGHT...
EVEN THIS HALBERD IS TOO LIGHT...
MY GOODNESS, YOU ARE A BIG STRONG APE! IT WEIGHS OVER 3,000 POUNDS!
BUT YOU MUST HAVE SOMETHING THAT WILL BE OF USE TO ME!
TAKE A LOOK FOR YOURSELF. I DON'T HAVE ANOTHER ONE LEFT! I SWEAR IT!
HMMM, SOMETHING IS SHINING OVER THERE!
OH, YOU BIG BEAST!... BUT BE CAREFUL OF THE RADIATION!
MY BEAUTIFUL DOOR OF SHELLS!

THAT IS THE ROD WITH WHICH THE MILKY WAY WAS FORGED AND LEVELED!
IT'S BEEN SITTING THERE FOR THOUSANDS OF YEARS, SHINING AND PALPITATING, AS IF IT HAS BEEN WAITING FOR SOMEONE. MAYBE YOU?
AND YOU SAY THAT THIS ROD WEIGHS MORE THAN 13,500 POUNDS? AND IT'S SOLID GOLD?
IT'S A BIT HEAVY... OH, WAIT... NOW THAT'S A GOOD FIT!
HEY, HOW DID YOU DO THAT? THAT ROD USED TO BE THREE MILES LONG! WHAT HAPPENED TO IT? WHO ARE YOU, YOUNG APE?
TIP TAP
DON'T YOU KNOW, DEAR DRAGON OF THE ORIENTAL SEA?
I SHALL NEED A HAT...
...AND POSSIBLY A LIVELY COSTUME... ONE OF THOSE SPANGLY KINDS. DON'T YOU THINK THAT WOULD FIT ME?

DON'T YOU EVER TAKE ANYTHING SERIOUSLY? YOU'RE DRIVING ME CRAZY! MAJORETTE... SMAJORETTE! NOW GO, I WANT YOU OUT IMMEDIATELY! I... I...
... I'LL WRITE THE EMPEROR OF JADE IF YOU DON'T LEAVE AT ONCE!
THAT'S WHAT I'LL DO. I'LL WRITE THE EMPEROR OF JADE!
dudu... i'm singing in the rain
WATCH THIS, LITTLE GIRL! EVERYONE, WATCH!
AND WILL THIS GOLDEN ROD BE YOUR WEAPON FOREVER? IT DOESN'T SEEM THAT WAY!
m. 29'657

ALL THE WAY UP HERE?
LOOK, IT'S THE YOUNG APE!
HE MUST HAVE CLIMBED UP HERE ON HIS NEW MAGIC WEAPON!
WEEKS AGO, HE WAS BOTHERING WITH HIS LIGHT TRICKS. NOW HE COMES TO JOIN OUR ORGY!
I AM IMMORTAL, YOU KNOW!
WOULD IT PLEASE YOU TO BE IMMORTAL, TOO?
NO, I DON'T WISH TO LIVE FOREVER! TOO LONG!
...HH...
Z
WHAT DO YOU SAY? DO YOU THINK THAT'S HIM?
NO DOUBT ABOUT IT! LET'S GET HIM!
HEY! WHERE ARE YOU TAKING ME?

KING
DEATH
SHIT! THIS IS THE KINGDOM OF YAMA- SAVIOR OF DEATH!
YEAH! AND YOUR TIME ON EARTH IS UP!
I'M IMMORTAL!
I AM NO LONGER MADE UP OF THE FIVE ELEMENTS!
STOK
GAAH!
I HAVE STUDIED, AND NOW I AM IMMORTAL! AND FRANKLY, I DON'T GIVE A DAMN ABOUT YAMA!
SGUOSH
EXCUSE ME, FELLAS... BUT I CAN'T DIE. THERE MUST HAVE BEEN SOME MISUNDERSTANDING!
UHOO
I WANT TO KNOW WHO THE HELL THIS GUY THINKS HE IS!
JUDGE OF LIFE AND DEATH! A GOD WITH A HAIRY FACE IS ENTERING YOUR CHAMBER. WHAT SHOULD WE DO?
LET HIM ENTER...

YOUR NAME, PLEASE?
HOW COULD YOU HAVE JUST SENTENCED ME TO DEATH, IF YOU DON'T EVEN KNOW WHO I AM?
WELL, A MISTAKE HAS BEEN MADE, BUT WE CAN'T PINPOINT IT. WE ARE LOOKING FOR SOMEONE BY THE NAME OF KING SOMETHING-OR-OTHER!
"MINISTERS CAN BE WRONG, AS CAN MAGISTRATES, BUT BAILIFFS ARE NEVER WRONG!"
WHAT A LOVELY PROVERB. DID YOU JUST MAKE THAT UP?
LET ME SEE THOSE BOOKS OF YOURS!
HMMMMM, LET'S SEE... BALD INSECTS, BLONDE INSECTS, WINGED INSECTS...
GIVE ME THAT!
IT'S NOT UNDER "APE," NOR IS IT UNDER "MAN"
LOOK ON PAGE 3,150.
"3,150"... LET'S SEE... "IMMORTALS... FATHER CHRISTMAS... TINKERBELL... CINDERELLA" YEP... ALL IMMORTALS! THERE!... "YOUNG APE OF STONE. IMMORTAL FOR THE DURATION." FOR THE DURATION???
WELL, SEE? I AM IMMORTAL. AND SO ARE THE MEMBERS OF MY TRIBE.
THANK GOD! THIS PLACE IS REALLY DEPRESSING!
IF ALL THE DEAD PEOPLE MADE THIS KIND OF FUSS...

A FEW DAYS LATER AT THE CHATEAU OF CLOUDS...
YOUR MAJESTY, THE DRAGON OF THE EASTERN SEA HAS A PROBLEM THAT HE WOULD LIKE TO TALK TO YOU ABOUT. HE IS RIGHT OUT-SIDE.
...AND... AND HE DE-MANDED MY WEAPON AND THEN SLAPPED ME. I HATE HIM. HE'S THAT AWFUL YOUNG APE!
HE IS A PROBLEM, ISN'T HE? I SENT HIM TO THE KINGDOM OF THE DEAD, AND HE CROSSED HIMSELF AND HIS WHOLE TRIBE OFF OF THE LIST OF PEOPLE WHO ARE SOON TO DIE.
YOUR MAJESTY, WITH ALL DUE RESPECT, WE DO HAVE A CONTRACT. THE APE CAN NOT ES-CAPE HIS EVENTUAL DOOM. IMMORTALITY IS A FALSE HOPE.
THIS YOUNG APE HAS BEEN A GREAT DEAL OF TROUBLE, I SEE!
YES. MY SAVIOR HAS HIT THE PROVERBIAL NAIL RIGHT ON THE HEAD.
HELP ME UP, CHILDREN.
WE MUST ARM A CELESTIAL TROOP OF 20,000 MINDS, IN ORDER TO SCATTER THIS IMPERTINENT YOUNG CHIMP INTO 20,000 LITTLE PIECES.
NO, WE MUSTN'T...
I, EMPERIOR OF JADE, SAVIOR OF ET CETERA, ET CETERA, ET CETERA, SAY TO YOU, THE DRAGON OF THE EASTERN SEA, TO RETURN IN SPITE OF YOUR MISHAP. RETURN TO YOUR KINGDOM, KNOWING THAT THE YOUNG APE WILL BE AVENGED. AND THE SAME HOLDS TRUE FOR YOU, CARETAKER OF THE KINGDOM OF THE DEAD.
DO YOU HAVE ANOTHER SOLUTION, MY DEAR INDIRA?

YES, YOUR MAJESTY. IF YOU CUT THAT ANNOYING LITTLE APE INTO 20,000 TINY PIECES, WE'LL HAVE 20,000 TINY AND VERY ANNOYING LITTLE APES! I PROPOSE THAT YOU PROMOTE HIM INSTEAD OF PUNISHING HIM. HE'LL HATE WORKING FOR YOU.

HMMMMM, AN INTERESTING THOUGHT. I LIKE IT!

HAVE HIM COME HERE. YOU CAN GIVE HIM SOME SORT OF BUSYWORK THAT'LL KEEP HIM OUT OF YOUR HAIR!
...IF I DIDN'T KNOW BETTER, I WOULD THINK YOU ARE INFATUATED WITH THE YOUNG APE.

AT DAWN...
SIGN HERE!
TOT TOT TOT

HMMM, AND I WAS JUST CONTEMPLATING TAKING A TOUR OF THE HEAVENS.

THANK YOU, O CELESTIAL ENVOY, FOR HAVING BOTHERED YOURSELF TO BRING THIS MOST INTERESTING MESSAGE.
THERE'S A MAN WHO IS HAPPY WITH HIS JOB!
SWWRROOM

NO SWEAT! I WAS DYING TO TRY OUT MY NEW MOTORCYCLE!
SWUiiS

...AND WITH HIS TOOLS OF MAGIC, THE YOUNG APE BUILT HIMSELF A MOTORCYCLE IDENTICAL TO THE ONE OF THE MESSENGER.

BYE-BYE, SLUG!!!
WAIT!

HOW DO WE KNOW THAT YOU ARE REALLY THE YOUNG APE?
I HAVE THE INVITATION HERE AS PROOF!

AND YOU KNOW WHAT THIS IS, DON'T YOU?
STOP!

YOU WERE SO EAGER TO GET HERE BEFORE ME, I DIDN'T HAVE A CHANCE TO WARN THE GUARDS ABOUT YOU... GO AHEAD IN, YOU MAY ENTER NOW... AND GET A HOLD OF YOURSELF.
TUMP
TUMP
TUMP

BOY, ANYONE CAN GET UP TO HEAVEN, NOWADAYS.
MAYBE HE GOT A GOOD RECOMMENDATION!
THEY PROBABLY JUST WANT HIM FOR SHOVELING HORSESHIT!

O POWERFUL EMPEROR OF JADE, WITH DILIGENCE...
ENOUGH! WHERE IS THE YOUNG APE?

WHAT TITLE SHOULD WE GIVE TO THIS APE?

THERE AREN'T ANY VACANT POSTS AVAILABLE RIGHT NOW! THE PORTFOLIOS HAVE ALL BEEN ASSIGNED. THERE IS AN OVER-ABUNDANCE OF UNDERSECRETARIES... AND WE HAVE A PLETHORA OF SUPER-BUREAUCRATS. WHAT ARE WE GOING TO DO WITH HIM?
MAKE HIM IMMORTAL IN-SPECTOR OF THE IMPERIAL STABLES! HOW DOES THAT SOUND TO YOU?

ANNOUNCING THE ARRIVAL OF THE IMMORTAL IN-SPECTOR OF THE IMPERIAL STABLES!
HMMM, I LIKE IT!

HEY, WHERE ARE THE HORSES?

SOMEONE PUT IN AN ORDER FOR THEM WITH REPORT NUMBER 51659 APL.
FINE! WHEN DID THE ORDER GO OUT?

OH, ABOUT 2,000 YEARS AGO... GIVE OR TAKE A FEW HUNDRED YEARS!

I BETTER TELL THE EMPEROR ABOUT THIS. THEY DON'T CALL ME THE IMMORTAL INSPECTOR OF THE IMPERIAL STABLES FOR NOTHING!

I'M GOING TO WRITE A RE-PORT ON THE PROB-LEMS HERE AT THE I.S. TRUST ME, GOOD AND DILI-GENT GROOMS, I'LL TAKE CARE OF EVERY-THING!

HEY, WHO ARE THEY?

MOST ILLUSTRIOUS...
EMINENT...
FASCINATING...
POWERFUL...
DEAR INSPECTOR OF THE IMPERIAL STABLES!
ENTHRALLING...
INFLUENTIAL...
EXCELLENT...
PERSONAL...
DISGUSTING...

HERE IS YOUR CHAIR, DEAR INSPECTOR! WE ARE WRITING YOU A REPORT ON THE PROBLEMS HERE AT HAND WITH THE I.S.

I DON'T UNDER-STAND...WHO ARE YOU?
WELL, THIS WHOLE THING EMANATES FROM THE PERSONNEL DEPARTMENT. WHENEVER THEY HAVE TO FIND A NEW POSITION FOR SOME-ONE, THEY MAKE HIM INSPECTOR OF THE I.S., FOR LACK OF A BETTER TITLE. NOW, PUT ON YOUR HAT, AND DON'T GIVE US ANY TROUBLE. OKAY?

WHO DO THEY THINK I AM?

THEY'VE GOT ANOTHER THING COMING!

THEY OBVIOUSLY AREN'T AWARE OF WHAT A TALENTED APE I AM! I HAVE SEVENTY-TWO TRANS-FORMATIONS AT MY FINGERTIPS!

OH, NO!

DO THEY REALIZE THAT I AM A KING? THAT I RIDE THE FASTEST CLOUDS OF AUGUSTE?

SKRASS

HALT! YOU ARE NOT ALLOWED TO LEAVE!
LET HIM GO! HE'S SUCH AN ASS!

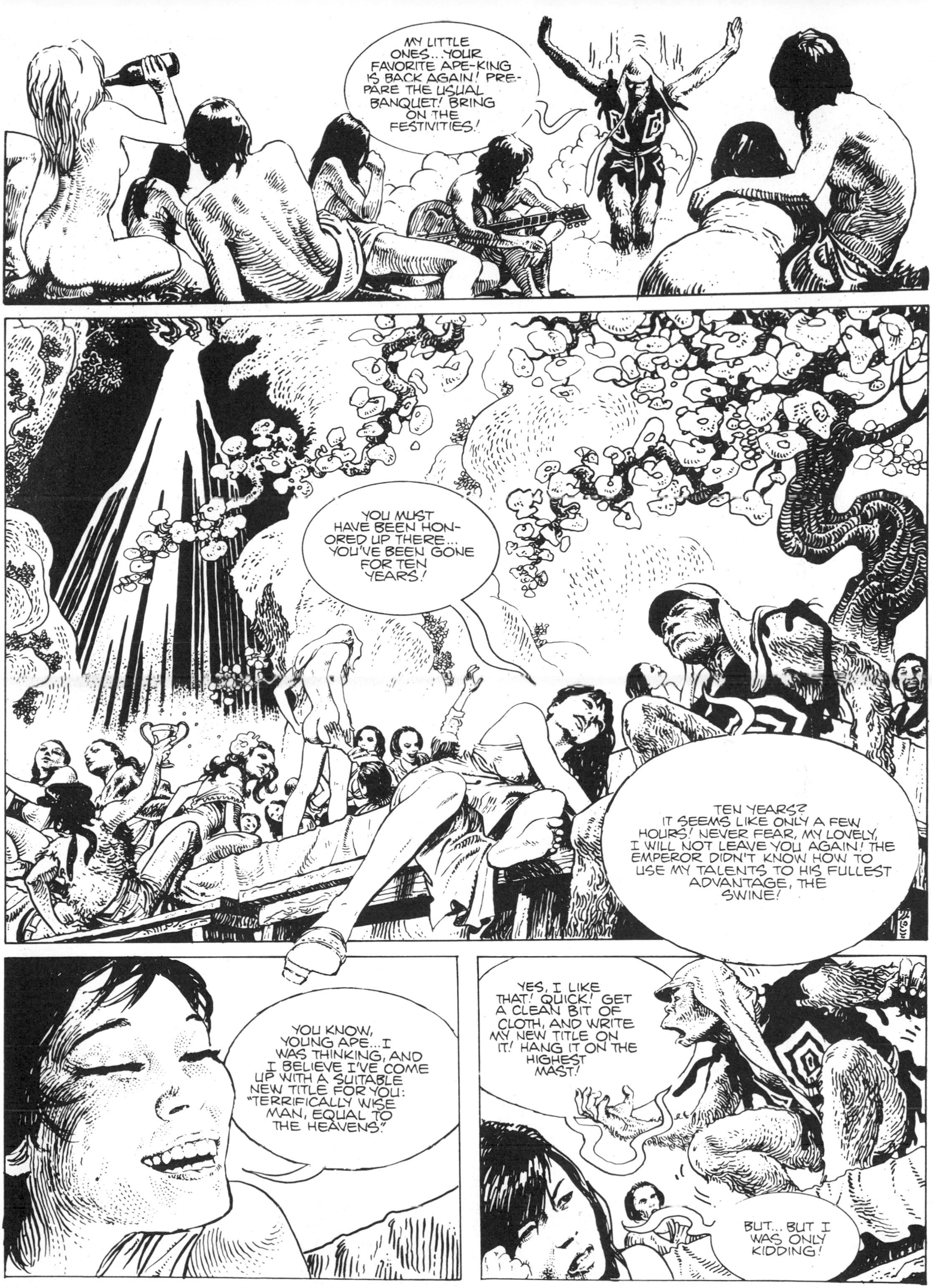

YOU MUST HAVE BEEN HON-ORED UP THERE... YOU'VE BEEN GONE FOR TEN YEARS!

TEN YEARS? IT SEEMS LIKE ONLY A FEW HOURS! NEVER FEAR, MY LOVELY, I WILL NOT LEAVE YOU AGAIN! THE EMPEROR DIDN'T KNOW HOW TO USE MY TALENTS TO HIS FULLEST ADVANTAGE, THE SWINE!

AND IN LESS THAN TEN YEARS THE CELESTIAL ARMY WAS READY. AT THE MOUND IS THE GREAT VAISRAVANA, IN RIGHT FIELD, HIS SON NATHA, LEFT FIELD, HIS BROTHER-IN-LAW, MAGIC SPIRIT, AND BATTING CLEANUP IS GENERAL FISH. WHAT A MIGHTY TEAM... WHAT AN ARMY!
"TERRIFICALLY WISE MAN, EQUAL TO THE HEAVENS!" HA HA... WHAT A LOW LIFE! HE COMES TO MY PALACE, WREAKS HAVOC IN THE CHAMBERS, DOESN'T ACCEPT THE TITLE I OFFER HIM... DO AWAY WITH HIM, MY CHILDREN!
BUT, PAPA... WHERE ARE YOU GOING?
I TOLD YOU, DON'T CALL ME "PAPA" IN FRONT OF THE MEN, YOU TWIT!
PICK A CARD... ANY CARD!

AND THE CELESTIAL ARMY IS OFF, HELL-BENT ON DESTRUCTION AND OTHER NOT-NICE THINGS. AS PER THE EMPEROR'S ORDERS–THEY ARE OUT TO GET THE YOUNG APE.
REJOICE, YOU DIRTY, BOORISH ASS. THE GREAT CELESTIAL ARMY IS HONORING YOU BY CAMPING OUT ON THE LAND WHICH YOU ARE CULTIVATING.
BUT, BUT MY CROPS...
YOU DARE TO PROTEST? POWERFUL MAGIC SPIRIT, KILL THIS MAN. HE IS UNDOUBTEDLY A COLLABORATOR!
NO! HAVE PITY!
CHOOSE A CARD, ANY CARD, BUT BE FOREWARNED– IF IT'S THE JACK OF SPADES...
...I'LL KILL YOU!
ZACCHETE
I'M DOOMED!
GOOD WORK, SPIRIT! NOW OFF YOU GO–TRY TO MEET WITH THIS YOUNG APE. IF WE CAN DO AWAY WITH HIM DURING A LITTLE ONE-ON-ONE, WE CAN SAVE A FEW THOUSAND SOLDIERS!

...AND WHEN THE POWERFUL MAGIC SPIRIT ENTERED THE YOUNG APE'S CHAMBERS...
不忘阶级
LET'S SOLVE THIS PROBLEM WITH A MAGIC TRICK. IF I WIN, YOU CONFESS THAT YOU HAVE INDEED BEEN CONQUERED AND I'LL CUT OFF YOUR HEAD. AND IF YOU WIN, YOU CONFESS THAT YOU'VE BEEN CONQUERED, AND I'LL ONLY CUT OFF YOUR TOES!
AH! WHAT A FORTHRIGHT PROPOSITION! I ACCEPT!
HERE'S ONE BALL... LOOK AT THE BALL... WHERE IS THE BALL? OOOPS... HERE IT IS... WATCH THE BALL... WHERE IS THE BALL NOW?
WHERE IS THE BALL NOW?
HERE!
PAM
PLINK PLINK
HE IS TOO STRONG FOR ME, VAISRAVANA. MY MAGIC IS NO MATCH FOR HIM!
MAGIC SPIRIT, YOU HAVE LET ME DOWN!
SEND ME, FATHER!
MY SON... WHAT A TWIT... WELL, I CAN'T REFUSE MY OWN FLESH AND BLOOD...
SO BE IT, MY BRAVE SON!

AH! LOOK AT WHAT A BEAUTI-FUL LITTLE BOY THEY HAVE SENT ME TO FIGHT! WHY, HE STILL HAS HIS BABY TEETH!
YOU REPULSIVE MONKEY! I AM THE THIRD SON OF VAISRAVANA! STRIKE NOW OR FOREVER HOLD YOUR PEACE!
HEYYYYY, MICROBE, BE CAREFUL WHEN YOU PLAY WITH SWORDS!
TRANSFORMATION!!!
WELL, LOOKEE HERE! WHO WOULD HAVE EVER THOUGHT THAT THIS LITTLE KID COULD DO THAT!

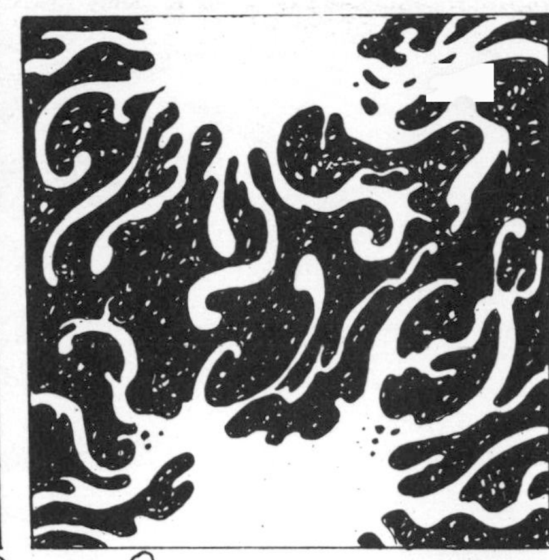

COME ON!
ATTACK!

TRANSFORMATION!
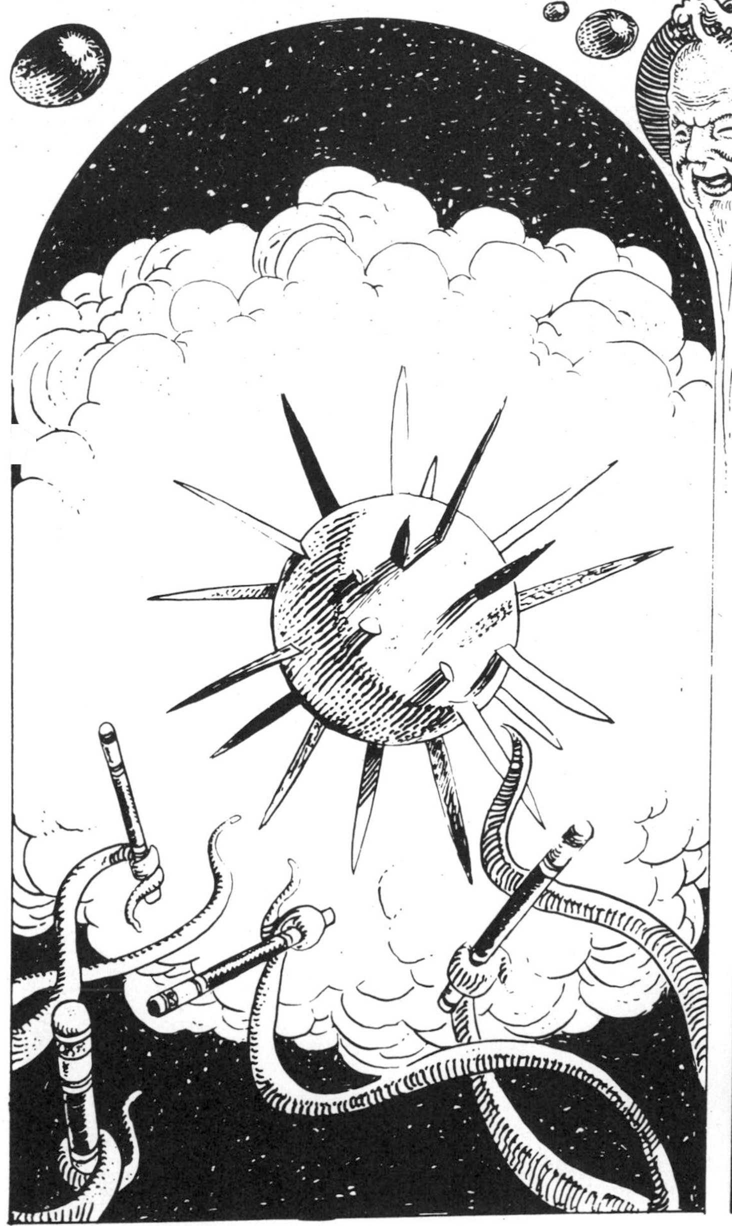

TRANSMATION!

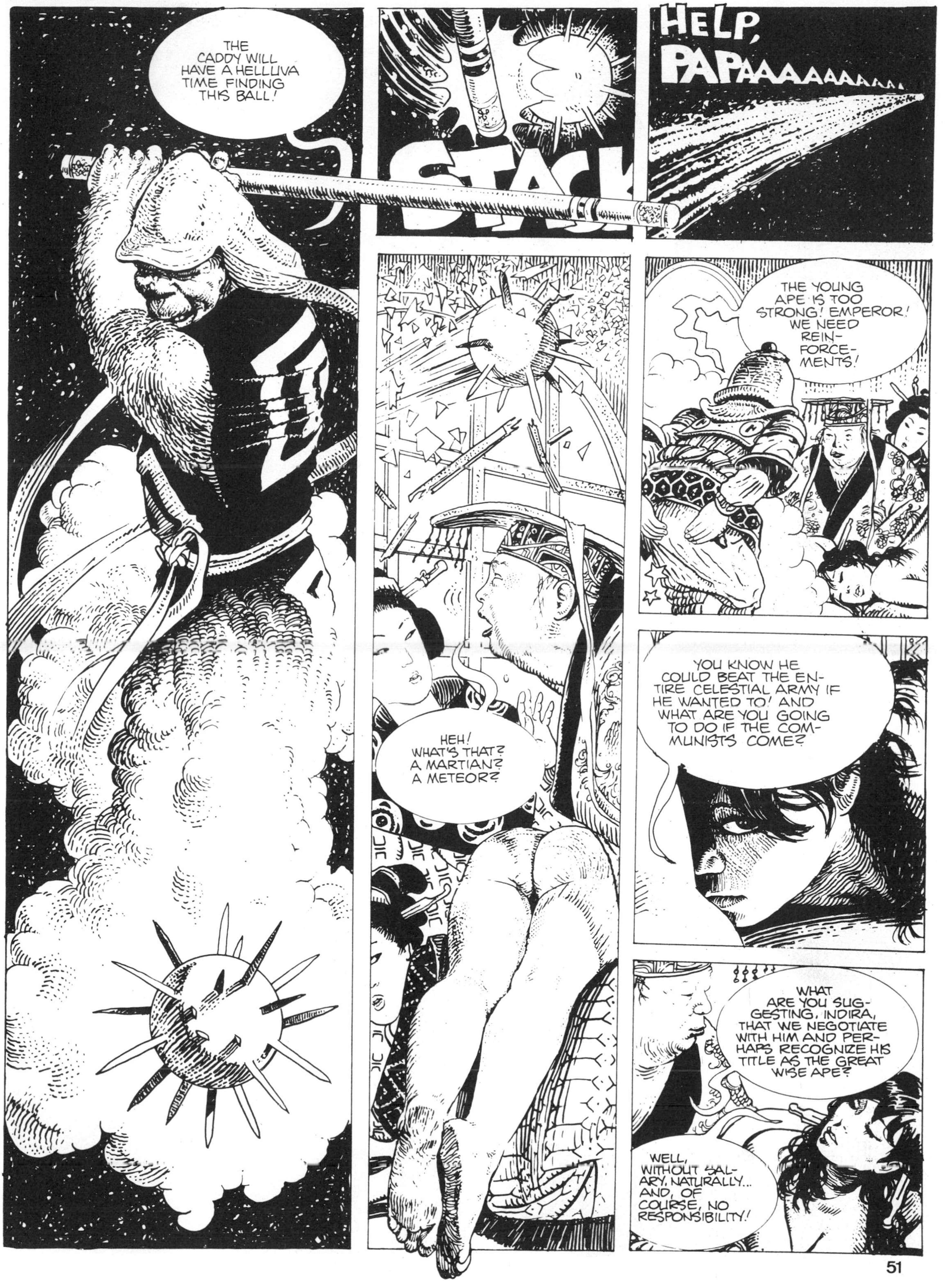

THE CADDY WILL HAVE A HELLUVA TIME FINDING THIS BALL!

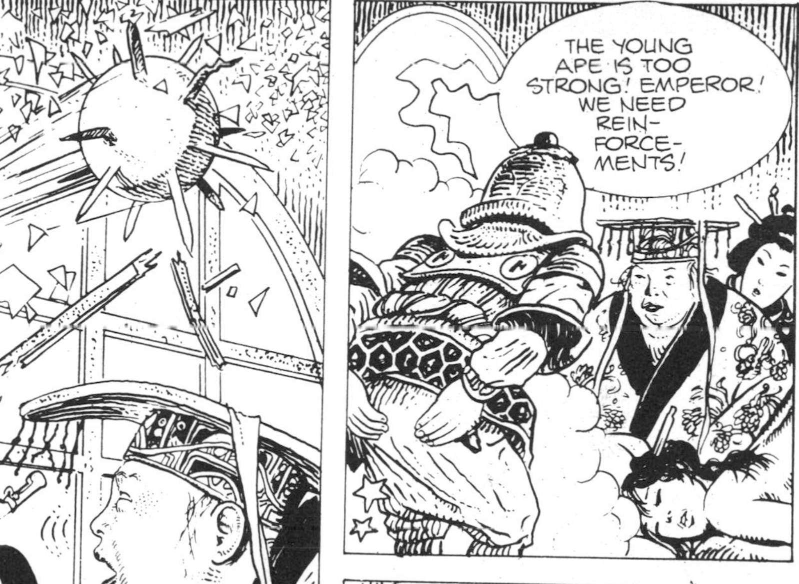

HEH! WHAT'S THAT? A MARTIAN? A METEOR?

IF THE PAY WASN'T AS GOOD, I'D QUIT! I CAN'T BELIEVE WHAT A HOLD THAT VULGAR APE HAS ON THE EMPEROR!
...YOU HAVE BEEN SUMMONED ONCE AGAIN. THIS TIME THE RED CARPET WILL BE ROLLED OUT FOR YOU.
IF YOU ARE LYING TO ME, I'LL DISMANTLE THE PALACE, BRICK BY BRICK, SET FIRE TO THE SACRED CLOUDS, AND BURY YOU UNDERNEATH THE WHOLE MESS!
WHAT A DRAG!
SO, WHAT DO YOU SAY? SHALL WE GO TOGETHER?
I'D LIKE THAT, BUT I HAVE NOTHING TO WEAR, EXCEPT THIS OLD RAG!
THE DAY OF ACCESSION...
YOUR GIRLFRIEND IS VERY ATTRACTIVE!
KEEP YOUR PAWS OFF OF HER, EMPEROR!

HMM, NICE GIRL... BUT SHE COULD BE DANGEROUS.
OH, I THINK THAT'S CONSCIENCE– THE YOUNG APE'S GIRL.

...SO THEN, MY YOUNG APE FRIEND, I PROCLAIM YOU A GREAT WISE MAN, EQUAL TO THE HEAVENS. THIS IS A GREAT AND NOBLE HONOR. I DO HOPE THIS WILL PUT AN END TO YOUR RUNNING AROUND, AND THE PLAYBOY IMAGE YOU SO ENJOY.

NO PROBLEM THERE, EMP. THANKS FOR THE GREAT TITLE!

THANK YOU...THANK YOU...THANK YOU...
THAT'S ENOUGH NOW. I'LL ACCOMPANY YOU TO YOUR QUARTERS.

AND THE GIRL THAT WAS WITH ME? WHERE DID SHE GO?
SHE WAS HERE A MINUTE AGO. WHO KNOWS WHERE SHE RAN OFF TO?

POOR GIRL...PROBABLY COULDN'T DEAL WITH MY FAME AND GOOD FORTUNE!

THE IDLE YOUNG APE WAS LEFT TO LIVE IN A SORT OF FALSE LIBERTY THAT HE HAD NEVER EXPERIENCED BEFORE. AND IF YOU THINK THAT HE'S GOING TO PUT UP WITH IT MUCH LONGER, JUST WAIT 'TIL YOU TURN THE PAGE!

WITH THE TITLE OF GREAT WISE MAN, EQUAL TO THE HEAVENS THE YOUNG APE HAS OBTAINED A GRAND PLACE IN THE PALACE OF JADE – THOUGH DULL IT MAY BE.
WHEN YOUNG APES DON'T HAVE MUCH TO DO, THEY BEGIN TO THINK – AND THAT'S WHEN THEY BECOME DANGEROUS.
YOU SAY I SHOULD PROMOTE THE YOUNG APE? WHAT'S HIS NAME? OH, YES, GREAT WISE MAN, EQUAL TO THE HEAVENS – WHAT A STUPID NAME!
DID YOU CALL FOR ME, MY DEAR AND TUBBY EMPEROR?
YES! FROM NOW ON, YOU WILL TAKE CARE OF THE PEACH TREE GARDEN. IT MUST ALWAYS BE SILENT THERE, AND NARY A PEACH SHOULD BE EATEN!
RISERVATO
RESERVED FOR THE SUPER OFFICE
HOW BEAUTIFUL IT IS HERE! BOY, WHAT ONE COULD DO WITH THIS PLACE... JUST A LITTLE INGENUITY AND A BIG SHOVEL. I COULD SEE A NICE AMUSEMENT PARK RIGHT ABOUT THERE!
THEY ARE VERY PRECIOUS AND HOLD IMMENSE POWERS! EAT JUST ONE OF THESE PEACHES AND YOU SHALL BE IMMORTAL!
HERE! WHY ARE ALL THESE TREES OFF LIMITS TO THE PUBLIC?

THEY RIPEN APPROXIMATELY EVERY 6,000 YEARS!
NOW I SEE WHY THE EMPEROR KEEPS THEM SO HIGHLY GUARDED.
RESERVED ONLY FOR THOSE WE L
YEARS OF SCANDAL, INJUSTICES, AND FLY-BY-NIGHT RELIGIONS INFILTRATE THE KINGDOM, UNTIL THE RICH PEACHES ARE...
RIPE!
Ripe!
RESERVED FOR SONS OF SECRETARIES
RESERVED FOR VETERANS!
QUICKLY, GARDENERS! GO GUARD THE GATES! NO ONE MUST ENTER NOR GATHER THESE FANTASTIC FRUITS!
WE'RE GOING... WE'RE GOING! GOD WISHES IT! WE WILL NOT LET A SOUL IN!
THE EMPEROR WOULD LIKE A HUGE FRUIT SALAD FOR DINNER TONIGHT. GO GATHER SOME RESERVED PEACHES, GIRLS!

STOP, COOK'S BEAUTIFUL GIRLS!
THE EMPEROR WANTS US TO PICK SOME PEACHES... AND WE MUST DO IT QUICKLY!
BUT...
...THEY HAVE...
...ALL...
...BEEN BITTEN!
HERE IS THE ONLY WHOLE ONE!
ONE LAST PEACH!
THE EMPEROR IS SUCH A SNOB, HE'LL NEVER EAT PEACHES THAT HAVE BEEN PARTIALLY EATEN! WE CAN ONLY BRING THIS ONE!
TRANSFORMATION
WHO GAVE YOU PERMISSION TO GATHER PEACHES THAT HAVE BEEN ENTRUSTED ONLY TO ME... YOU, YOU EVIL MONSTERS!?!
THE EMPEROR IS GIVING A FEAST TONIGHT! HE WANTS THE CHEF TO MAKE A GRAND FRUIT SALAD! WE HAVE COME ON OFFICIAL BUSINESS!
A BANQUET, HUH? AND WHY HAVEN'T I RECEIVED AN INVITATION YET? I'M GOING TO SEE ABOUT THIS! WAIT FOR ME HERE!
WELL, DON'T CALL US MONSTERS! WE WERE ONLY FOLLOWING ORDERS!
AH, YES! THE YOUNG APE CAN FREEZE MAIDENS INTO A TREE WITH HIS SECRET POWERS! A LITTLE BIT OF THIS, AND A PEPPERING OF THAT AND VOILA!

THE PALACE BANQUET QUARTERS WERE STILL EMPTY!

HOW WILL I KNOW IF I HAVE BEEN INVITED IF THE GUESTS HAVEN'T EVEN ARRIVED YET!
SNIF SNIF

POWER
SPLASCH
TILT
I KNOW 72 TRANSFORMATIONS... I KNOW HOW TO FLY... I AM IMMORTAL... SO I'LL BE ABLE TO LAP UP A FEW LITERS OF ELIXIR AND NO ONE WILL BE THE WISER!

HMMM, THERE HE IS. OLD LAO-TSENE DISTILLING HIS ELIXIR! I WONDER WHAT DIPAN-KARA, THE BUDDHA OF THE PAST IS DOING HERE? THE AROMA IS SIMPLY MARVELOUS!
ELISIR dell'imperato

TRANSFORMATION!

IS THE ELIXIR READY? I WANT TO MAKE A GOOD IMPRESSION AT THE PARTY THIS EVENING.
YES, POWERFUL EMPEROR. EVERY-THING IS ACCORDING TO YOUR SPECIFICATIONS!

HIC

SMACK

EMPEROR?
WHAT?
BRRRRR!

THE JUG IS COMPLETELY DRUNK!
AND IRREVERENT, NO LESS!
HMMM, HE REMINDS ME OF SOME-ONE!

CALL ERH-LANG, CHIEF OF THE EMPERIAL POLICE. TELL HIM WE WANT TWO MEN DOWN HERE AT ONCE TO GET RID OF THIS DRUNKEN WHATEVER-IT-IS!
LOOK, DON'T ARGUE WITH ME. I'M ONLY A MESSENGER. THE EMPEROR WANTS YOU DOWN THERE TO GET RID OF SOME DRUNK!
THEY MUST HAVE FLIPPED THEIR CROWNS UP AT THE CHATEAU OF THE CLOUDS! THIS IS A JOB FOR US!
YES, CHIEF! WHICH ONE DO YOU WANT, THE SILVER OR THE RED?
DID YOU TAKE THE DEVIL'S REFLECTIVE MIRROR?

THEY'RE FINALLY COMING! THANK GOD!
I BEG YOUR PARDON, DEAR?
BUT I KNOW THAT MAN...
FREE THE FALCONS AND FORM A CIRCLE!
HIC... LITTLE BIRDS FLYING HIGH, WHY DO YOU DROP ON ME FROM THE SKY... HIC!
TRANSFORMATION!
DRINK AND DEFEND YOURSELF... THEY WANT TO CUT YOU UP INTO 20,000 LITTLE PIECES... FOR A CHANGE.
THANK YOU, AUNTIE!
HERE YA GO. NEXT TIME, DON'T BOTHER US WITH LITTLE NUISANCES LIKE THIS FILTHY APE!
HEY, WAIT A MINUTE!
TRANSF
ION

BUT... BUT THEY'RE BREAKING EVERY-THING!
THE YOUNG APE IS WINNING TEN TO ONE.
DONE!

UTILIZING HIS MAGICAL AND TRANSFORMATIONAL POWERS, THE POWERFUL ERH-LANG FIGHTS OUR YOUNG APE, WHILE THE ENTIRE COURT OF THE CHATEAU OF THE CLOUDS WATCHES ON. MANY PREFER TO WATCH THEM ON THE NEWLY-INSTALLED CABLE STATION.
COULD YOU MOVE A LITTLE MORE TO THE RIGHT... A LITTLE MORE... THERE, THAT'S FINE. I CAN EVEN SEE THE DROPLETS OF SWEAT WITH THE ZOOM!
BUT, YOUR MAJESTY, THEY'VE BROKEN EVERY PIECE OF THE PORCELAIN CHINA SERVICE.
GIVE HIM A SWING WITH YOUR RIGHT, YOUNG APE.
STOP RIGHT THERE FOR A CLOSE-UP.
WITH PLEASURE. ONE MUST ALWAYS BE AGREEABLE WITH THE PRESS.
SOCK
THIS KIND OF THING NEVER HAPPENS AT THE OLYMPICS.
I'VE WON! YEAH! NOW I'LL PURSUE HIM AND CUT HIM INTO LITTLE PIECES!
YEAH, WE KNOW, WE KNOW... INTO TWENTY THOUSAND LITTLE PIECES.

THIS GUY IS STRONG, EVEN FOR ME. I'D BETTER HIGH-TAIL IT OUT OF HERE, BUT QUICK.
LADIES AND GENTS, THE YOUNG APE HAS LEFT THIS HAPPY GET-TOGETHER. THE GROUP CONTINUES ON, BUT ERH-LANG FOLLOWS, HOT ON HIS FURRY HEELS.
FORWARD, MY DEAR BRAVE ONES... TO THE YOUNG APE!
NO!!!
CALL THE IMPERIAL ARCHITECT! I WANT THIS PLACE RECONSTRUCTED WITHIN THE NEXT TWO DAYS— DOWN TO THE LAST TEACUP!
MAYBE IN A NICE ROCOCO STYLE, MAIS OUI?
WHAT A CHIC IDEA, MY DEAR! ROCOCO IT IS, THEN!
I'LL HIDE IN THE POND— MAYBE DISGUISE MYSELF AS A FISH!
TRANSFORMATION!
THERE HE GOES! NOW THAT THE FISHING SEASON IS CLOSED, I'D BETTER DISGUISE MYSELF AS A CORMORANT— DON'T WANT TO BREAK THE LAW.
AS YOU CAN SEE, THE FISH HAVING A DIP OVER THERE IS THE YOUNG APE. HE'S THE ONLY HAIRY FISH IN THE POND!
WHO DOES HE THINK HE'S KIDDING? I KNOW THAT THAT CORMORANT IS REALLY EHR-LANG! WHAT A NIT!
TRANSFORMATION!

HMMM. WHERE HAS HE HIDDEN?
GUIT
GUIT
AH HA! NOW HE'S TRANS-FORMED HIMSELF INTO A BUZZARD, THE LOWEST AND MOST DETESTABLE OF ALL POSSIBLE TRANSFORMATIONS!
LADIES AND GENTS, WE ARE BACK AGAIN WITH THE CONTINUED DUEL BETWEEN EHR-LANG THE CORMOR-ANT, AND THE YOUNG APE THE BUZZARD. THE BUZZARD IS KNOWN FOR ITS NYMPHOMANIACAL WAYS: FRANKLY, IT WILL SCREW ANYTHING THAT COMES INTO REACH.
YOUR TURN!
BUT... BUT... IT REALLY WAS A BUZZARD!
WELL, WHAT DID YOU THINK IT WAS? A HAMMERHEAD SHARK?
YOUNG APE? YOOHOO! WHERE HAVE YOU HIDDEN YOURSELF?
I'VE SEEN QUITE A FEW SANC-TUARIES IN MY TIME, BUT NONE WITH A HAIRY FLAGPOLE!

I DON'T LIKE THIS SANCTUARY. I THINK I'LL THROW A ROCK IN THE WINDOW...

...AND THEN I'LL KICK THE DOOR IN.

SHIT! THE DOOR IS MY MOUTH, THE WINDOWS, MY EYES. IF HE BREAKS MY TEETH, AND GOUGES MY EYES OUT, NO RESPECTABLE GIRL WILL EVER FALL IN LOVE WITH ME AGAIN.

TIGER'S LEAP STRAIGHT UP TO THE SKY.

SO, DID YOU GET HIM?
HE WAS HERE A MINUTE AGO. HE TRANSFORMED HIMSELF INTO A SANCTUARY. BUT THERE WAS A RUMBLING AND NOW HE'S GONE.

DID YOU FOLLOW HIM WITH YOUR CABLE WHATCHAMACALLIT?
LET'S SEE. I THINK I CAN GET HIM ON THIS CHANNEL. THERE...

AS YOU CAN SEE, THE YOUNG APE IS PEDDLING QUICKLY, 75 MILES AN HOUR, TO BE EXACT. AND WITH AN EASY AND ELEGANT TURN OF THE HANDLEBARS, HE'S HEADING TOWARDS THE ESTUARY OF THE RIVER OF LIBATIONS, AND THE FLYING STAGE.
BU... BUT THAT'S MY PALACE.
UNFORTUNATELY, THE VIDEO CONTACT HAS BEEN INTERRUPTED BECAUSE OF THE FLYING STAGE. ALL THE SAME, WE'LL FOLLOW OUR YOUNG APE, WHO FINALLY WISED UP, AND HAS TRANSFORMED HIMSELF INTO EHR-LANG.
TRANSFORMATION
GOOD EVENING, AND WELCOME, MASTER!
ERRR, YES. HERE I AM. DID THE PLEBES DOWN BELOW BURN A LOT OF INCENSE WHILE I WAS GONE?
COUGH... COUGH... YEAH, I GUESS THEY DID. YOU CAN LEAVE NOW, MY CHILDREN.
BUT... THERE ARE NO CHILDREN HERE!
GOOD! AND DON'T START MAKING ANY, EITHER!
IN THE MEANTIME, THE REAL EHR-LANG RETURNS.
IT'S ME, YOUR BOSS! I'M BACK!
INSIDE THERE IS AN EHR-LANG, AND BELIEVE YOU ME, ONE BOSS IS ENOUGH. THEREFORE, YOU CAN NOT COME IN.

OH, POWERFUL EHR-LANG! THERE IS ANOTHER EHR-LANG OUTSIDE!
NOT OUTSIDE ANY LONGER. HERE I AM!
MOTHER, WHAT A MESS!
YOUNG APE, YOU'VE OVERSTEPPED YOUR BOUNDS THIS TIME!
ONE MINUTE! I MUST TELL YOU ONE THING. THIS SANCTUARY WAS CONSECRATED BY THE GOD OF THE...
APES?
...APES!
eeeeEEAAIIIIOO
ARGH
THERE HE IS!
BOY, THEY'VE BEEN FIGHTING ALL DAY LONG!
EHR-LANG IS NOT DOING TOO BADLY.
THE ARMY WAS BETTER BEFORE.
NOW THEY'RE BLUDGEONING HIM!
GO! COME! HERE! THERE! FORWARD! BACK!

THEY'LL NEVER GET HIM! HE'S TOO STRONG!
WHAT IF WE THREW A VASE ON HIS HEAD? HE'D FAINT, AND THEN WE COULD TRAP HIM ALIVE!
I THINK I'D BETTER TAKE CHARGE.
LAO-TZE, FOUNDER OF TAOISM... DO YOU HAVE A WEAPON?
I HAVE BUT A SIMPLE LASSO OF DIAMONDS, AS YOU CAN SEE. WHEN I LEFT CHINA TO CONVERT THE BARBARIANS OF THE WEST, THIS CAME IN VERY HANDY. HERE, TRY IT!
WHAT IS THAT... A KITE?
A MAGICAL LASSO... THERE'S NOTHING I CAN DO ABOUT IT... I CAN'T EVEN TRANSFORM MYSELF!
VICTORY! WE'VE WON! LONG LIVE EHR-LANG!
WHO ARE THEY KIDDING? EHR-LANG, THE CONQUEROR OF ME? IF IT WASN'T FOR LAO-TZE, HE WOULD NEVER HAVE CAPTURED ME.
IT'S NOT IMPORTANT WHO CAUGHT YOU. JUST AS LONG AS I GET THE CREDIT, WHO CARES?
EXACTLY! LET'S TAKE OUR LITTLE HAIRY BUNDLE BACK TO THE EMPEROR!

ZAK
YOU STAY AND BURY THAT INSUB-ORDINATE BROTHER OF YOURS AND I'LL DELIVER THE APE TO HIS MAJESTY AND GET ALL THE CREDIT.
GOT YOU LOUD AND CLEAR, BROTHER!
HAVE A GOOD TRIP!
CONQUER CONQUER CONQUER AND WE'VE CONQUERED IN THE SKY ON EARTH AND ON SEA
THAT SONG IS VERY NICE. HAS IT MADE THE TOP TEN YET?

AS PRISONER OF THE CELESTIAL TROOPS, THE YOUNG APE IS TAKEN TO THE EXECUTION SITE WHERE HE WILL MOST LIKELY BE CUT UP INTO 20,000 LITTLE PIECES. NOT ONE MORE, NOT ONE LESS.

HEY, THIS IDEA OF THE STARS AND THE ELECTRICAL BOLTS IS TERRIFIC. SORT OF LIKE SHIATSU. HMMM... A LITTLE TO THE LEFT, PLEASE.
IT'S USELESS. HE'S IMPERVIOUS TO THE "FIVE STARS," TOO.
MASTER, I HAVE NO IDEA WHERE HIS INVINCIBILITY COMES FROM.
YES, INDEED. HE IS EXTRAORDINARY WITH ALL OF HIS MAGICAL TRICKS.
YOU KNOW, WHEN YOU THINK ABOUT IT, IT'S NOT SO EXTRAORDINARY AFTER ALL. HE DID EAT ALL OF THOSE IMMORTALITY PEACHES ...AND HE DID DRINK THE ELIXIR OF LONG LIFE! THOSE THINGS ADD UP WHEN IT'S A QUESTION OF DYING!
HMM, FIVE FULL BOWLS OF ELIXIR IN THAT SHORT AMOUNT OF TIME. I DOUBT WE'LL EVER BE ABLE TO CONQUER HIM. BRING HIM TO MY LABORATORY AND LET ME SEE WHAT I CAN DO.
I COMMAND THAT THE YOUNG APE, GREAT WISE MAN, ETC..., BE BROUGHT TO LAO-TZE, INVENTOR OF ETC..., FOR FURTHER INSPECTION, ETC...
MASTER, FOUNDER, NOT INVENTOR. GRANTED, A TECHNICALITY, BUT AN IMPORTANT ONE, NONETHELESS.
INDIRA, I LIKED IT BETTER WHEN YOU WERE STUPIDER THAN I.

MY DUCE!
DON'T CALL ME THAT! SO YOU WANT TO BE REWARDED FOR COMBATING THIS UNCHAINED FURRY FURY THAT CALLS HIMSELF THE YOUNG APE?
HERE'S YOUR RETRIBUTION!
100 FLOWERS OF GOLD!
100 MOTHBALLS!
100 JARS OF CELESTIAL WINE!
PLUS A LARGE QUANTITY OF PEARLS AND BROCADES BROUGHT TO YOU BY BOXER AND BOXER, "JEWELERS TO THE CLOUDS."
FOR LACK OF ANYTHING BETTER TO DO WITH HIM, THE YOUNG APE IS PLACED IN A LARGE VAT OF ALCHEMICAL FIRE.
MAKE SURE THE FIRE IS KEPT ALIVE. AFTER FORTY DAYS HE WILL BE REDUCED TO ASHES. ALL THAT WILL BE LEFT IS A FEW DROPS OF ELIXIR.
SA MA EL LI LITH
WOULD YOU MIND LOWERING YOUR HEAD? I HAVE TO CLOSE THE CONTAINER.
TENTH DAY: LOSS OF HAIR.
TWELFTH DAY: THE SKIN'S GOING QUICKLY.
THIRTIETH DAY: BONES ARE ABOUT ALL THAT'S LEFT.
FORTIETH DAY: I'LL GET THE ELIXIR: YOU THROW OUT THE ASHES.
OPEN THE CRUCIBLE, MY LOVELY AIDS!

SPSFFF
OOOH, THE LIGHT. THAT REALLY HURTS MY EYES. SURPRISE, BOYS AND GIRLS!
LONG LIVE FREEDOM!!
YOU! BUT YOU'RE SUPPOSED TO BE ASHES. THE ALCHEMIST'S FIRE SHOULD HAVE CONSUMED YOU.
GET LOST, LAO-TZE, AND SAY A HOWDY-DO TO TAOISM FOR ME!
AIUTOOO
I'M GOING TO RUN AMOK THROUGH THIS PALACE SO QUICKLY THEY WON'T KNOW WHICH WAY IS UP AND VICIE-VERSIE!

NOT AGAIN!
MASTER, THE APE DID NOT EXPIRE IN THE CRUCIBLE AFTER ALL. I DON'T KNOW WHAT COULD HAVE GONE WRONG!
YYAARRU
TOK
LEAVE HIM TO ME!
LOOK HERE, ZORRO. YOU DIDN'T THINK YOU COULD STOP ME WITH THAT WHIP, DID YOU?
EHR-LANG SHOULD BE FIGHTING THIS CREEP, WHAT WITH ALL THOSE GOODIES HE RECEIVED FROM THE EMPEROR.
LET'S GO INTO THE CONFERENCE ROOM. I MUST TRY TO SUMMON BUDDHA. HE IS OUR LAST HOPE.

OH GOD
I REALLY MUST TAKE A ROMP UP TO THE CHÂTEAU OF THE CLOUDS!
CAN YOU TALK A LITTLE LOUDER? YOU ARE SUCH A BOTHER! YOU TURN EVERYTHING UPSIDE-DOWN— AND THAT'S WITH TWO Ds!
HEY, DON'T EXAGGERATE THE PROBLEM AT HAND.
MY DEAR BUDDHA, DON'T UNCURL YOUR YOGA POSITION ON MY ACCOUNT!
MASTER, HAVE YOU NOT HEARD ABOUT THE YOUNG APE'S ESCAPE?
HELP!

REST, MY CHILDREN! YOU, LITTLE APE, COME HERE!
WHAT KIND OF BOZO ARE YOU? DON'T BOTHER ME IN THE HEAT OF BATTLE!
I AM THE BUDDHA OF THE WESTERN PARA-DISE, AND YOU? WHERE DO YOU COME FROM? SINCE WHEN DID YOU POSSESS ILLU-MINATION? AND WHY DO YOU CAUSE SUCH HAVOC EVERY-WHERE YOU ROAM?
I AM THE YOUNG "MAGIC" APE FROM THE MOUNTAIN OF FLOWERS AND FRUIT. I AM IMMORTAL AND ABLE TO CHANGE MYSELF INTO MANY DIFFERENT SHAPES, SIZES, AND BEINGS. NOTHING SATISFIES ME MORE THAN LIVING IN THE HEAVEN OF GREEN JADE. I HATE THE CROWDED SURROUND-INGS MAN HAS BECOME ACCUSTOMED TO.
SAINT PATIENCE! AREN'T YOU AN EVIL APE? WHAT IS IT EXACTLY THAT YOU WANT?
I WANT...
WELL, WHAT DO YOU WANT? I'M SURE I DON'T KNOW!
WELL, IF I CAN'T BE KING, I WANT THE SECOND BEST THING. BEING THE HERO OF ALL TIME WILL SUIT ME JUST FINE!

HAHAHA! YOU'VE AIMED TOO HIGH, MY LITTLE NUBBLY FRIEND! GIVE UP AND I'LL LEAVE YOU WITH WHAT FEW POWERS YOU NOW POSSESS.
THERE IS A PROVERB WHICH STATES...
TODAY IS THE EMPEROR OF JADE'S TURN... TOMORROW IS YOURS.
SO...
STRAK
GO AHEAD, BUDDHA! TELL THE EMPEROR TO MOVE ON AND LEAVE ME HIS THRONE. THE HAND OF POWER IS ITCHING ME.
LET'S SEE WHAT MAGIC TRICKS YOU POSSESS THAT WOULD MAKE YOU WORTHY OF THE KINGDOM BLESSED BY THE HEAVENS?

THIS BUDDHA GUY DOESN'T KNOW WHAT HE'S IN FOR! HASN'T HE HEARD OF THE YOUNG APE'S TRANSFORMATIONS ?
DO YOU HAVE A FEW DAYS? I CAN HANDLE ABOUT 72 TRANSFORMATIONS. AND IF THAT ISN'T IMPRESSIVE ENOUGH, I CAN JUMP— IN ONE SINGLE LEAP, MIND YOU— 80,000 YARDS... MAYBE A LITTLE MORE.
SO, YOU WANT TO PUT A LITTLE MONEY DOWN ON THIS?
JUMP OVER THE PALM OF MY HAND!
IF YOU ARE ABLE TO, I WILL TELL THE EMPEROR OF JADE TO COME AND LIVE IN MY PALACE, AND YOU CAN HAVE HIS. IF YOU CAN'T... OH, WOE TO YOU!
THIS BUDDHA IS A COMPLETE IDIOT... UNLESS, OF COURSE, THIS IS SOME SORT OF A TRICK! THE PALM OF HIS LEFT HAND MUST BE APPROXIMATELY TWENTY CENTIMETERS. THERE SHOULDN'T BE ANY PROBLEM.
OKAY. I ACCEPT.

YYEAAAA
THE BUDDHA WATCHED THE YOUNG APE. HE WAS APPARENTLY AMUSED BY THE CHILDLIKE INNOCENCE OF THIS FURRY PERFORMER.
E=mc²
I'M SOARING! READY TO LAND, WITH ROOM TO SPARE, I BET!
HERE, THIS IS WHERE THE WORLD ENDS. WHAT A GREAT JUMP!
NOW ALL I HAVE TO DO IS GO BACK AND CLAIM MY PRIZE FROM THAT BAG OF FLESH! OH, WAIT A SECOND!

I'D BETTER LEAVE A MARK SOMEWHERE, JUST IN CASE THEY NEED PROOF!
I MADE IT
OOOH, I GOTTA GO...GOTTA GO! NO ONE WILL EVER KNOW THE DIFFERENCE IF I TAKE A LEAK RIGHT HERE.
TAKE THAT... EHEHEH!
HMMM, I WONDER WHERE MY CORONATION WILL TAKE PLACE.
HERE I AM! I WON!
YOU STINKING, IRREVERENT FURBALL!
OOOPS!

YOU'VE BEEN ON MY MIND THE WHOLE TIME!

COME ON, BUDDHA! I WENT AS FAR AS THE BOUNDARIES OF THE WORLD! THERE WERE FIVE PILLARS OF PINK, AND THE MIDDLE ONE I WROTE...

"I MADE IT."

I MADE IT

BUT... BUT HOW COULD THIS BE?

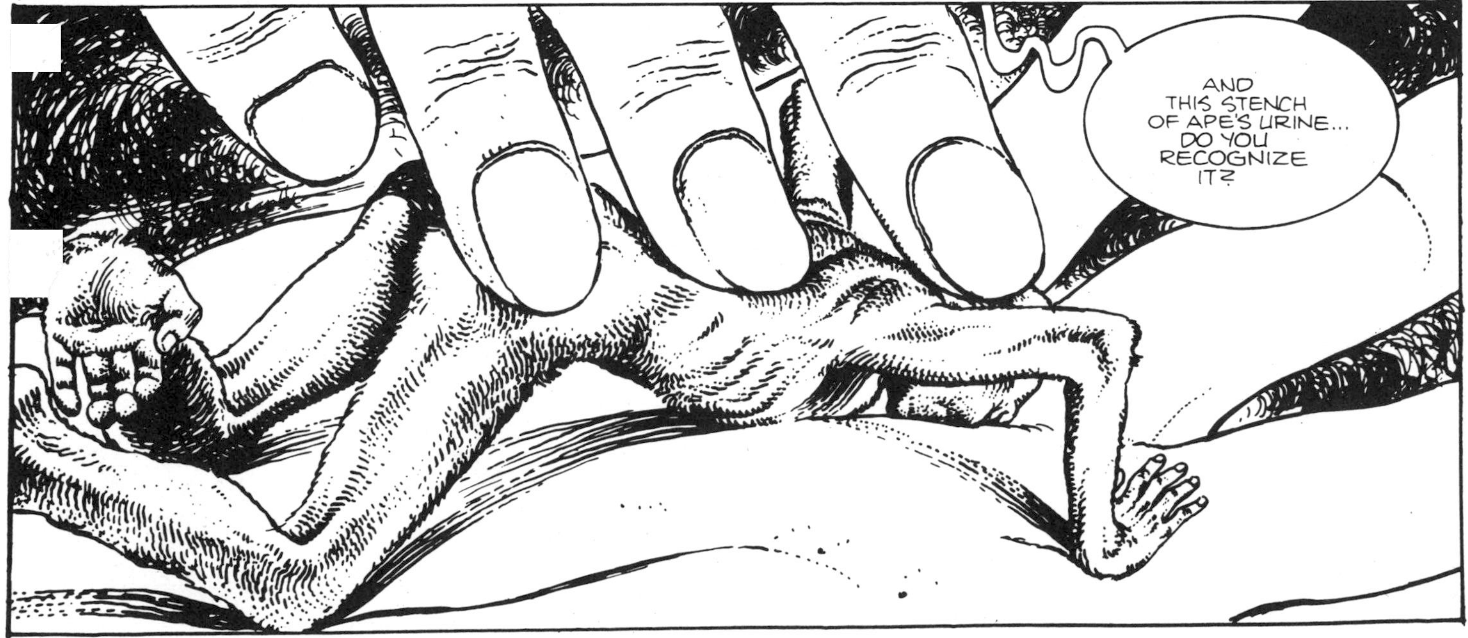
AND THIS STENCH OF APE'S URINE... DO YOU RECOGNIZE IT?

LET MY FINGERS TURN INTO THE FIVE ELEMENTS... METAL... WOOD... WATER... FIRE... EARTH! THEY SHALL FORM A MOUNTAIN, AN ETERNAL PRISON!
SANGEMINI
ACQUA MI
NOOO

AT THE GROTTO OF DYING WATER... AT THE BASE OF THE MOUNT- AIN OF FLOWERS AND FRUITS... NOT ONE MONTH LATER...
COME ON! TAKE OFF THE BLACK BAND!
WE HAVE TO GO ON IN HIS NAME! WE CAN'T BURN EVERYTHING OF HIS!
ARE THEY ALL HERE?
WHO KNOWS? FOR THE MOMENT, THE LIST INDICATES WE HAVE FORTY-FOUR, PLUS THESE FOUR. AFTERWARDS, WE'LL ROUND UP ANY NEW SUSPECTS!
WHERE ARE YOU TAK- ING ME?
NO COMMENT!
HOWEVER, AT THE CHÂTEAU OF THE CLOUDS IN THE DIZZINESS OF THE PETALS AND THE ODOR OF THE INCENSE, THE BANQUET HONORING BUDDHA, THE CONQUEROR OF THE YOUNG APE, COMES TO AN END.
THE CREDIT DOESN'T BELONG TO ME, BUT TO TAO. AND THE OTHER DIVINITIES.
DON'T BE SO MODEST, OH POWERFUL BUDDHA! WITHOUT YOU, WESTERN AND CELESTIAL ECONOMY WOULDN'T HAVE HAD A CHANCE. NOW I CAN HOLD OUT MY HAND AND HARVEST!
MR. BUDDHA- MAN? PERHAPS IT IS THE WINE TALK- ING, BUT I COULD SWEAR THAT THE MOUNTAIN MOVED DOWN BELOW!
ME, TOO. I SAW IT, ALSO. IT WAS LIKE A TREMOR!

IS IT STILL MOVING? NO MATTER! TAKE THAT AND SEAL HIM INSIDE!
LEAVE A SMALL SPACE SO HE CAN GET HIS AIR SUPPLY! IF HE'S HUNGRY, GIVE HIM AN IRON PILL. IF HE'S THIRSTY, A COUPLE OF DROPS OF NECTAR SHOULD DO! THAT SILLY LITTLE CHIMP SHAN'T BOTHER US ANY LONGER!
IRON AND NECTAR. YES, DOCTOR!
FORUNATELY, SHE'S STILL HERE!
THAT'S HER, SHE'S ALWAYS CRYING!
THEY FREED HER A MOMENT AGO. SHE'S COMING FROM THE MOUNTAIN OF FLOWERS AND FRUITS!
LET'S GO THERE, THEN!
NO! NOO! NOOOO

A LITTLE BLOOD IS LEFT ON THE SEAL!
THAT'S NOTHING! THAT'LL BE THE PROOF THAT SNOW WHITE IS REALLY DEAD!
PACIFISTI
INTELLECTUALS OF SHIT
WORKING CLASS
PACIFISTS
EVERYTHING IS DONE WITH
DISILLUSIONMENT
ROLE OF THE INTELLEGUALS
STILL A FEW MORE MONTHS
CONTINUE THE NEUROTIC FIGHT
WHICH ONE WAS THE YOUNG APE?
LUMUMBA
PINELLI

THE END